I'm going to read

UP TO
50
WORDS

I'm Going To READ!

These levels are meant only as guides;
you and your child can best choose a book that's right.

Level 1: Kindergarten–Grade 1 . . . Ages 4–6
- word bank to highlight new words
- consistent placement of text to promote readability
- easy words and phrases
- simple sentences build to make simple stories
- art and design help new readers decode text

Level 2: Grade 1 . . . Ages 6–7
- word bank to highlight new words
- rhyming texts introduced
- more difficult words, but vocabulary is still limited
- longer sentences and longer stories
- designed for easy readability

Level 3: Grade 2 . . . Ages 7–8
- richer vocabulary of up to 200 different words
- varied sentence structure
- high-interest stories with longer plots
- designed to promote independent reading

Level 4: Grades 3 and up . . . Ages 8 and up
- richer vocabulary of more than 300 different words
- short chapters, multiple stories, or poems
- more complex plots for the newly independent reader
- emphasis on reading for meaning

Note to Parents

What a great sense of achievement it is when you can accomplish a goal! With the **I'm Going To Read!**™ series, goals are established when you pick up a book. This series was developed to grow with the new reader. The vocabulary grows quantifiably from 50 different words at Level One, to 100 different words at Level Two, to 200 different words at Level Three, and to 300 different words at Level Four.

Ways to Use the Word Bank

- Read along with your child and help him or her sound out the words in the word bank.

- Have your child find the word in the word bank as you read it aloud.

- Ask your child to find the word in the word bank that matches a picture on the page.

- Review the words in the word bank and then ask your child to read the story to you.

Related Word Bank Activities

- Create mini-flash cards in your handwriting. This provides yet another opportunity for the reader to be able to identify words, regardless of what the typography looks like.

- Think of a sentence and then place the mini-flash cards on a table out of order. Ask your child to rearrange the mini-flash cards until the sentence makes sense.

- Make up riddles about words in the story and have your child find the appropriate mini-flash card. For example, "It's red and it bounces. What is it?"

- Choose one of the mini-flash cards and ask your child to find the same word in the text of the story.

- Create a second set of mini-flash cards and play a game of Concentration, trying to match the pairs of words.

LEVEL 1

Library of Congress Cataloging-in-Publication Data Available

4 6 8 10 9 7 5 3

Published by Sterling Publishing Co., Inc.
387 Park Avenue South, New York, NY 10016
Text copyright © 2006 by Harriet Ziefert Inc.
Illustrations copyright © 2006 by Tanya Roitman
Distributed in Canada by Sterling Publishing
c/o Canadian Manda Group, 165 Dufferin Street
Toronto, Ontario, Canada M6K 3H6
Distributed in Great Britain and Europe by Chris Lloyd at Orca Book
Services, Stanley House, Fleets Lane, Poole BH15 3AJ, England
Distributed in Australia by Capricorn Link (Australia) Pty. Ltd.
P.O. Box 704, Windsor, NSW 2756, Australia

I'm Going To Read is a trademark of Sterling Publishing Co., Inc.

Printed in China
All rights reserved

Sterling ISBN 13: 978-1-4027-3092-4
Sterling ISBN 10: 1-4027-3092-6

For information about custom editions, special sales, premium and
corporate purchases, please contact Sterling Special Sales
Department at 800-805-5489 or specialsales@sterlingpub.com.

I'm Going to Boston to Visit the Ducks

Pictures by Tanya Roitman

Sterling Publishing Co., Inc.
New York

I'm going to Boston.

I'm going to Boston
to visit the ducks.

What?

I'm going to visit
the ducks.

What ducks?

I'm going to visit
the ducks in the garden.

garden

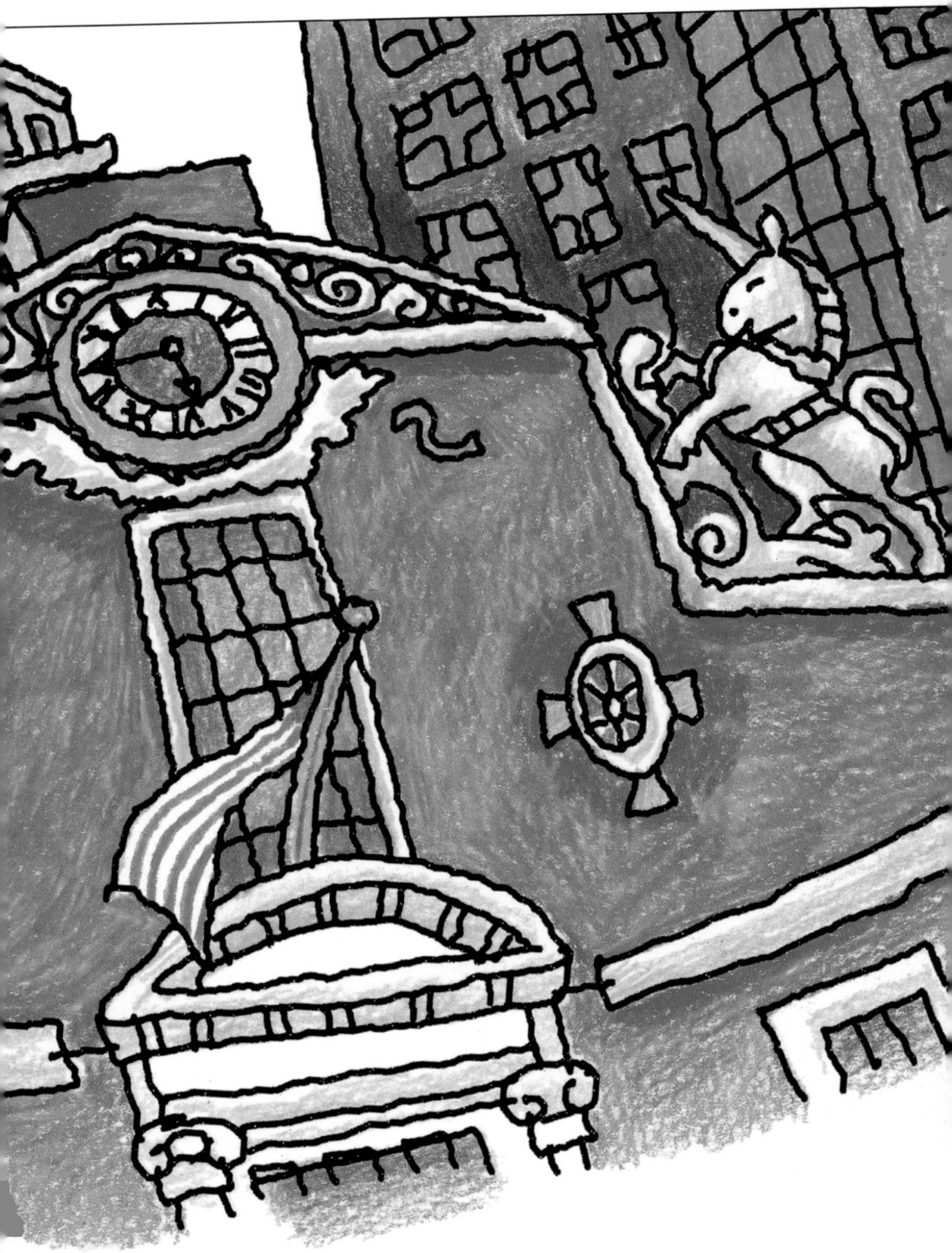

What garden?

public

The Public Garden!

Are those the ducks?

No. Those are not ducks.
Those are swans.

And those are
the swan boats.

geese

Are those the ducks?

No. Those are not the ducks.
Those are the geese
who live in the Public Garden.

Are those the ducks?

Yes! Those are the ducks.

Jack, Kack, Lack,
Mack, Nack,

Ouack, Pack, and Quack
are the ducks.

I'm touching the ducks.
First Jack, second Kack,
and third, Lack.

Then Mack, then Nack,
then Ouack, and then Pack.
And last . . . QUACK!

Would you like to visit
the ducks in Boston?